choughins

this book belongs to

. . . . . . . . . . . . . . . . . . . . . . . . . . . . . . . . . . . . . . . . . . .

Felicity Tattersall

Published by choughins

choughins is an imprint of Tor Mark Ltd,
United Downs Industrial Estate,
Redruth, Cornwall TR16 5HY

www.tormark.co.uk

Published 2021

ISBN 978 0 85025 100 5

Printed and bound in the UK

# Cornish Mice

# & the Treasure Garden

Written and Illustrated by Felicity Tattersall

choughins

Do you like it when the sun shines? Do you love that feeling of warmth on your skin, and how the colours sing in the sunshine?

Me too.

This story begins in a garden where the sun isn't shining.

"It's like a piece of the jigsaw is missing!" said Ronnie. The magical Treasure Garden was absolutely glorious in the summer but this year something was very wrong.

Ronnie, (a small brown garden mouse) and his younger sister, Isla, didn't understand.

On this day, the garden creatures studied the skies, muttering to one another.

Something was very wrong.

The most **GIGANTIC** tree you could imagine stood in the centre of the Treasure Garden, like a marquee mast keeping the roof up. Bigger than the tallest mountain on earth, the tallest leaves almost touched the overland above our sky. This ancient tree, called Osmunda, was a temperamental old grump whose moods dictated the weather in the garden, which could change from snow to sunshine to showers in the snap of a branch.

Mr Robin was just leaving Ronnie and Isla's house. He delivered messages around the garden but was extremely forgetful.

He frequently lost his spectacles and his tummy was so round, it looked like a cherry.

He hopped out of the mouse nest expectantly, but his shoulders drooped, "Very grey again" he said to himself, dropping letters into the rhododendrons.

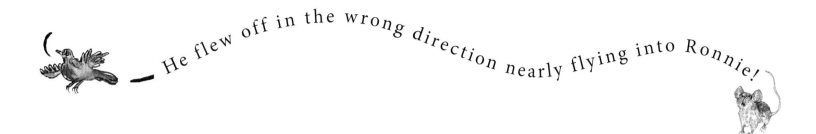

He flew off in the wrong direction nearly flying into Ronnie!

Recovering himself mid-flight, Mr Robin called over his shoulder "See you at the harvest party on Tuesday!"
"I think you mean the Spring Fair on Saturday!" corrected Ronnie, with a smile.

Everyone knew that Mr Robin would turn up for a birthday party on Thursday.

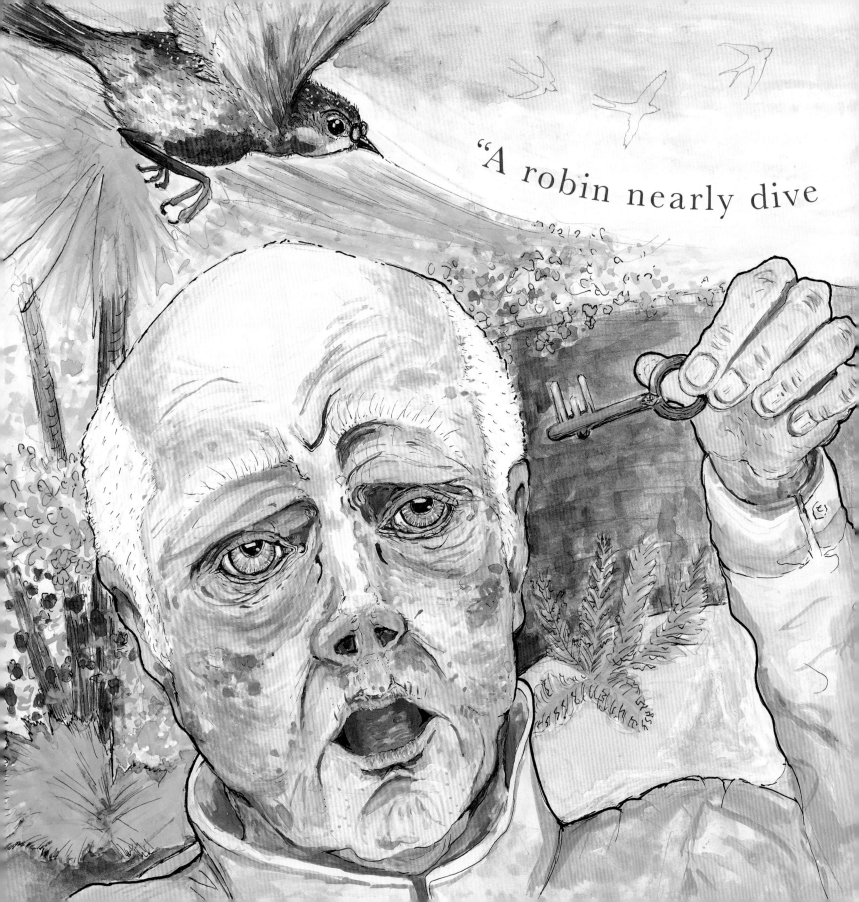

"A robin nearly dive

"bombed me!"

Exclaimed William, a white haired man who looked after the big house when the family were away.

He kept his head down in case of more flying ambushes. He was over seventy and walked with a stoop. Today he had the impossible task of matching up a box of lost keys.

The keys all fitted into a lock somewhere in the garden. Sometimes even the keys themselves seemed to disappear before he could match them.

He blew the dust from the next key and examined it closely. It had a tiny green stone set into its bow but the door it fitted had disappeared. No matter how hard he tried, he couldn't find the right door.

William sucked in his top lip. "Every garden has its secrets", he said to himself with a toothless smile, "but this old place even more so".

Below ground, Martha the hedgehog yawned and stretched as she shuffled her snout out of her cosy nest into the sunless garden. She was extremely shy and only visited the garden at night to practice her singing.

Martha emerged into a glittering sky.
She admired the fairytale ballerina magnolia trees.
Passing the mineral-speckled hydrangea petals,
she spied a little lonely leaf lying on the
ground and noticed something strange. Shapes had
been deliberately torn away to make words.

Martha read them s l o w l y ...

FIND WHAT MAKES THE

SUN SHINE

Martha was worried, this was serious.
By sunrise the leaf had been taken
by the wind.

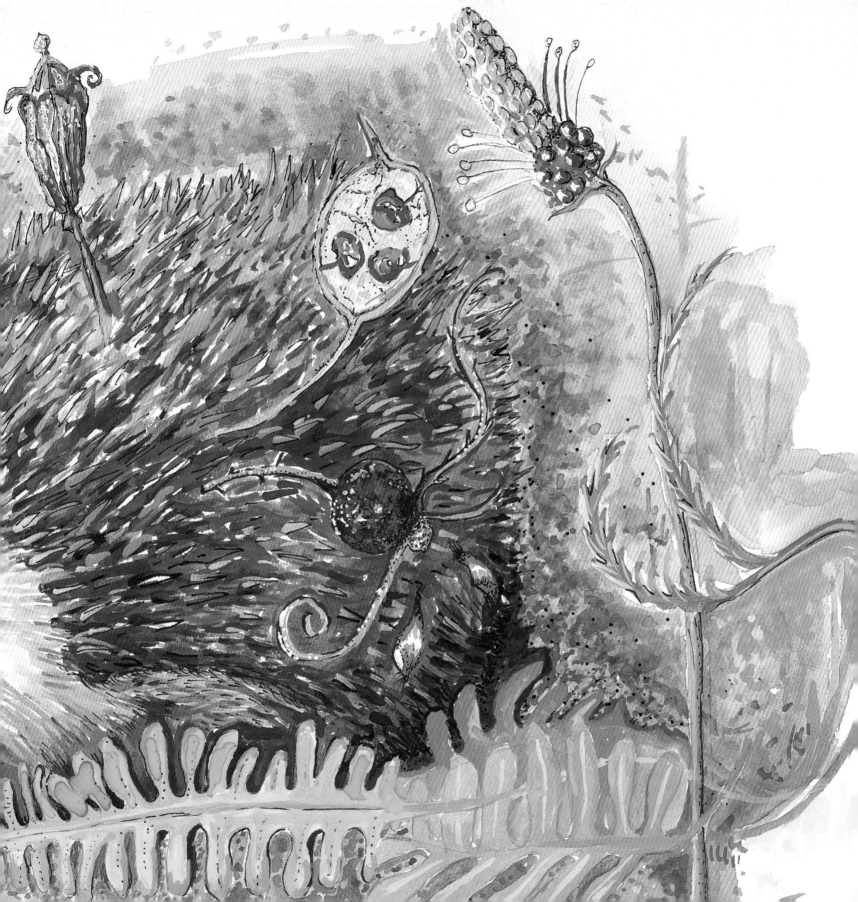

The daffodils were trying to open in the chilly April air. The garden creatures gathered around Osmunda's vast roots sending up pleas for sunshine.

Osmunda rudely ignored them and pretended to be asleep, occasionally letting out an **enormous** snore.

Martha knew that Osmunda needed different minerals in the soil to create the weather balance in the garden.

Only Martha understood that if Osmunda was missing one of his minerals, the weather would start to behave oddly. Martha knew more about nature than anyone else because of her secret, she was a potion-maker.

She collected plants, roots, sap and seeds as she shuffled around the garden at night, spearing them onto her spines, and making them into healing potions.

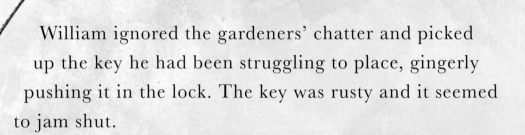

The next day the gardeners told William that a mysterious door had been found in one of the walled gardens behind a waterfall of ivy. He hobbled off taking his box of keys, eagerly hoping for one less key to match up.

William ignored the gardeners' chatter and picked up the key he had been struggling to place, gingerly pushing it in the lock. The key was rusty and it seemed to jam shut.

Eventually, with a lot of j *i* g g l i *n* g, it turned and clicked.

The door creaked open a fraction.

Suddenly, his concentration was shattered by a "bbbrrring bbbrrring". With a humph of annoyance, William hastily trudged back to the big house to answer the telephone. In his haste, he dropped the smaller key with the green stone in its bow and cheeky Mr Robin made a swift dive for it.

He picked up the key and quickly flew off.

Meanwhile, Ronnie and Isla had been walking to the orchard to collect foxgloves for Martha, and had watched the discovery of the new door. They peeked warily around it.

There was nothing to see apart from an overgrown, unloved little garden, with a birch tree in the middle. At the bottom of the tree lay a scroll of thin bark. Isla, being far braver than Ronnie, threw caution aside and scurried straight over to it.

She unrolled it and read out the words...

# FIND THE MIRROR TWIN, SHE HAS THE ANSWERS!

Isla signalled for Ronnie to come over and look. He didn't like the writing one bit. His tummy felt a bit upside-down.

They took the scroll and decided to show it to Martha.

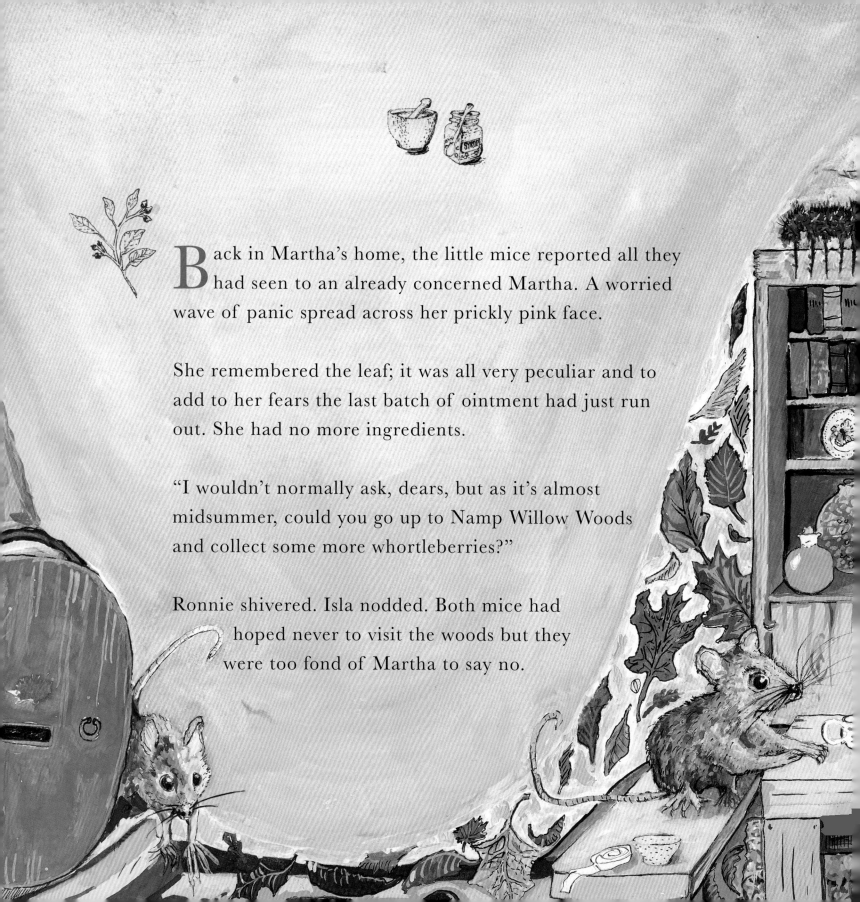

Back in Martha's home, the little mice reported all they had seen to an already concerned Martha. A worried wave of panic spread across her prickly pink face.

She remembered the leaf; it was all very peculiar and to add to her fears the last batch of ointment had just run out. She had no more ingredients.

"I wouldn't normally ask, dears, but as it's almost midsummer, could you go up to Namp Willow Woods and collect some more whortleberries?"

Ronnie shivered. Isla nodded. Both mice had hoped never to visit the woods but they were too fond of Martha to say no.

"We can do this Ronnie," said Isla forcefully, dragging her brother by the paw towards the dark shadowy woods which towered over them like a ghostly cathedral.

Ronnie's teeth were c h a t t e r i n g.

They tried to creep in noiselessly, but tawny owls **HOOTED** announcing their arrival.

Tall shadows moved across the woodland floor which was covered with wood sorrel.

"We should go back. Mum and Dad will be worried," said Ronnie authoritatively.

"We are NOT letting Martha down," whispered back the loyal Isla, fiercely.

"Don't give up so easily"
said an eerie voice croakily.

Ronnie
and Isla froze, unable
to move. "Look under that birch
tree," the voice continued. Ronnie
shook with fear, but Isla found the courage
to search underneath. She collected pawfuls of
the juiciest inky berries. All the time, they knew they
were being watched. Those eyes belonged to the Sea
Witch of Namp Willow Woods, part witch, part spirit,
who could inhabit any plant. "Not many come here,"
she continued whilst considering the two little mice
carefully. "But bravery is always rewarded. I'm
going to tell you about the mirror
twin, because she holds the
secret."

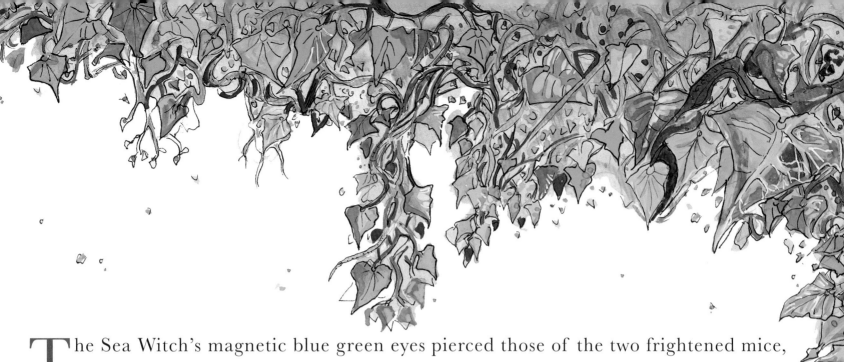

The Sea Witch's magnetic blue green eyes pierced those of the two frightened mice, who desperately wanted to escape back to their beloved garden.

The Sea Witch had inhabited a tree's vast root network. She started chewing her own tendril thoughtfully, then spat it out as she began. "She is a little girl, but the seriousness of one so young strikes you first. No laughter in those stern eyes. She would only be about five years old but is dressed like a grown up. Her childhood stolen from her. Her eyes are pools of endless charcoal grey. She was one of twins, the shadow twin."

"Trapped between this world and the overland, she only exists in reflections. She carries a small mirror at all times. It is cracked and silvered with age but with that mirror she moves between worlds using the reflection in the overland to transport her."

"Find her," she whispered.

Ronnie and Isla scurried back to the garden, climbing over rocks and through towering grasses. How were they to know where to start?

For what seemed like an age, they searched high and low throughout the garden, avoiding the human family.

Defeated and weary, they sat down against the walled garden tumbling with wisteria.

The nobbled and twisty stems suddenly turned into witch's fingers and started to grow beside poor Ronnie's head.

Too terrified to move, he simply let out a tiny squeak. The fingers signposted them towards the bridge.

As they scurried at top speed towards the bridge, Isla's eyes fixed on the lily pond.

At once she saw the mirror twin trapped in the water. Her face was feather white.

Luckily Martha was nearby when the mice shouted to her.

"We need your help!"

Martha took a big breath, making her bristles stand on end and started to sing.

The mirror twin seemed to come alive. Colour seeped into her cheeks for the first time. She took out her mirror and held it up for them to watch.

A chest was being opened. "Where is that?" questioned Isla.

The mirror went cloudy, then it showed a boat. "It's no good if we don't know where that boat is," shouted Ronnie impatiently.

The mirror twin shook her head sadly; she couldn't speak. But she could draw.

The air seemed to whiten as she drew a map of the garden. Finally, she drew a cross in the waters surrounding the garden, and wrote the word 'Miranda'.

"The Miranda is in the lead," announced one of the gentlemen proudly.
The air was salty with excitement as the family watched the boat race. They didn't notice two tiny mouse silhouettes scoot right in front of them on the lowest step.

Out of breath they rested for a second under some daisies. "Come on, Ronnie!" Isla hissed. Just then Mr Robin flew over them. "Have you seen anything out in the bay?" Isla shouted up to Mr Robin.

"Yes, what was it now?" he mused, concealing the key beneath his wing.
"Please remember!" screeched Ronnie.

Mr Robin puffed his chest out a few times and scratched his nose. He was tapping his foot and mouthing the letter

'M'.

Ronnie nearly tore his hair out in frustration when a tiny stray shard of sunlight fell onto Mr Robin's head. Very suddenly and clearly he said "I remember. It was a boat. Yes, sailing past the beach. The Miranda."

HALFWAY
MARKER

Their throats dust dry and chests throbbing from running so hard, Isla and Ronnie arrived at the beach, splashing and squelching through the mud.

They could see the Miranda out on the water. She was in front by several lengths.

How on earth could they get onto a

moving boat?

They needed help and looking upwards they saw the mirror twin with a small boat.

She was beckoning them to get in, but how could they?

The mirror twin held up her mirror, and fixed it on the two mice, shining a ray of reflected sunlight down to collect them.

The mice were lifted up and transported towards her bright white boat.

On deck, Isla hauled up the anchor and the boat surged forward, in pursuit of the Miranda.

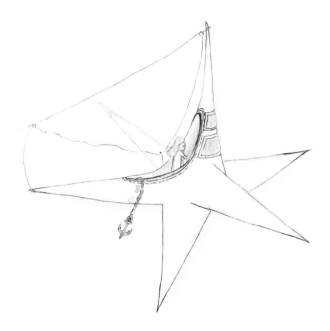

The cloud waves jostled the boat and spray whipped Isla's face. Ronnie's arms ached from pulling at the ropes but he didn't have time to complain.

Just as they reached the point in the overland, directly above the Miranda, the mirror twin smiled for the first time. Isla beamed back at her, and a very seasick Ronnie managed a weak smile.

She nodded and smiled, before gently lowering them down onto the bough of the Miranda and back into their world. The crew were cheering and singing loudly, celebrating their victory in the race.

Ronnie and Isla  c r e p t  below deck.

**M**r Robin was was being called by a bigger force from beyond the garden.

He took off, w o b b l i n g and flew down over the fields, over the beach and across the water...

...until he
spied his landing spot.

Circling to enable a better landing, Mr Robin touched down on the

bobbing Miranda.

Ronnie and Isla saw the chest in the corner. Creeping towards it they tried to lift the lid, but it was no use. It was locked and they couldn't see the key.

A moment later, Mr Robin flew down and offered the key in his beak to Ronnie. Placing it into the lock, the lid opened and a powerful bright green phosphorescent light shone from the gems inside the chest.

Left behind on the beach, Martha sighed with relief as the Miranda appeared, swishing through the water, before mooring near the beach.

Carefully, Ronnie and Isla began moving the gems onto the beach, one at a time.

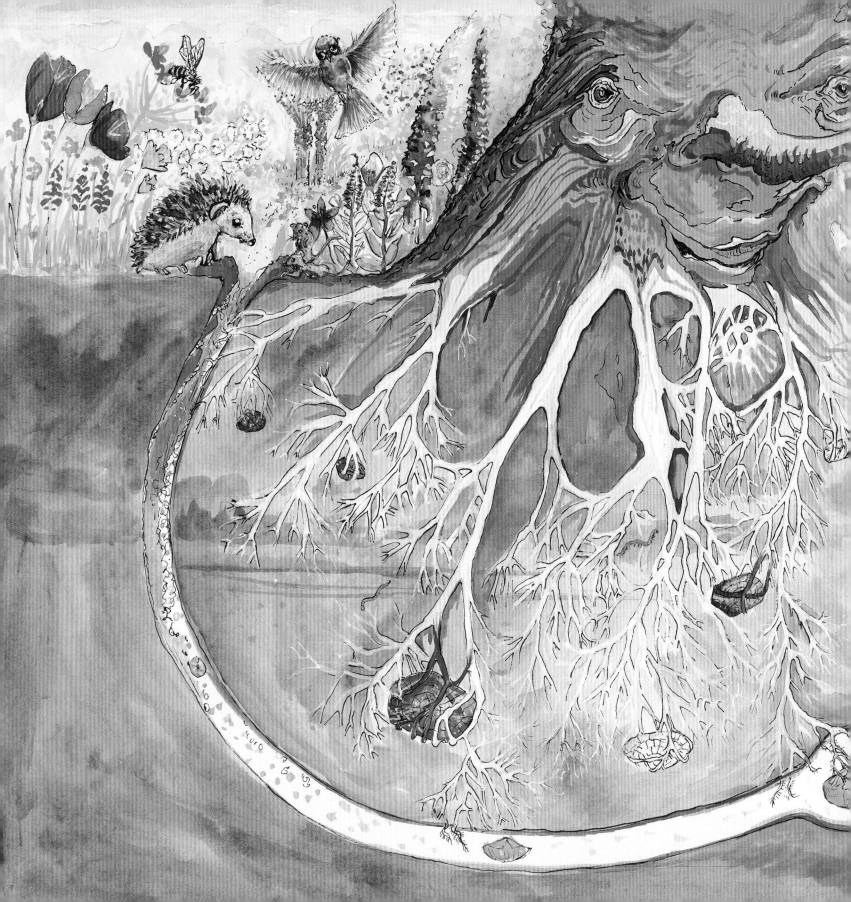

The two exhausted mice had one last task before bed. All the garden creatures gathered around Osmunda in the late afternoon.

As they dug down they found Osmunda's thread-like roots, and in amongst these tangled white whiskers were tiny gems of jewel-like stones in all colours and hues except green.

Slowly, they planted the green nuggets, blanketing them in their bed with warm soil.

The line where Osmunda's mouth would have been, started to

turn up into a smile.

Suddenly a yellow light brightened until it glowed. "No greater treasure than sunshine," said Mr Robin, as sunlight tickled the ears of all of the creatures. His words echoed around the garden as buds blossomed into flowers.

The garden was covered in *buttercups*

The animals were surrounded by musky, woozy, honeyed scents.

And the sound of bees filled the garden.